# A BRAVE
# LITTLE PRINCESS

written by
### BEATRICE MASINI

illustrated by
### OCTAVIA MONACO

walk
the way of wonder...
**Barefoot Books**

Once upon a time there lived a princess who was very beautiful, but also very small. In fact, she was so small that when she was four years old, she looked as if she was only two. And now that she was eight years old, she looked as if she was only six.

When she passed by on her pony, the other children whispered, "She's as small as a mushroom," or "She's as small as a blade of grass."

And the gardeners said, "She is as small as a bonsai," which is a miniature tree.

And some nasty people said that she was too small to be a real princess, because real princesses were tall and elegant.

They said it quietly so that no one could hear them. But they were not quiet enough. The princess heard what they said, and it made her sad.

One day Little Princess Leonora – for that was her name – went
to find the Queen Mother, who was not only her grandmother but
also her best friend.

Little Princess Leonora threw herself into her grandmother's
arms and asked, "Why am I so small? And why does everyone
make fun of me?" And the Queen Mother replied, "They do it
because they don't know any better. Your grandfather was small,
just like you, but he was a great hero all the same."

"What did he do?" asked the little princess.

"He set out from here with his army and defeated all our enemies
so that now our country lives in peace," replied her grandmother.

"I want to do something brave!" said Little Princess Leonora.
"I want to go on an adventure all by myself."

The Queen Mother thought about this for a long time.

"Very well," she said at last. "But if you are going to travel alone,
you had better take these."

And she gave Little Princess Leonora some useful things for
her journey:

a bow and arrow to protect herself against enemies;

a gold coin, just in case;

a comb and a mirror so that she could brush her hair;

and three candies to cheer her up.

Then the Queen Mother set her granddaughter's crown on her
head, gave her a kiss...

...and Little Princess Leonora set off.

She made her way through three forests, she climbed over two mountains, and she crossed a lonely desert. After many days, she came to a village where all the people were being terrorized by an enormous dragon. They were so afraid that they stayed hidden inside their houses. They didn't even dare set a foot outside.

But Little Princess Leonora was not in the least bit afraid.

"I can fight the dragon with my bow and arrow," she said to the mayor. "Look!"

But the bow and arrow only looked like toys.

"They are too small," sighed the mayor.

"Not for me," said the little princess.

Then she took the bow and pulled back the string, just as she had seen the Queen Mother's archers do. Everybody stared at her and she heard them whispering, "She is so small, she will never be able to kill the dragon."

But Little Princess Leonora refused to give up. She climbed the mountain where the dragon lived, and shot a little arrow, which pierced the beast right in the middle of its enormous stomach.

"Ahhh!" cried the dragon. "How my stomach hurts!"

Then the little princess strode up to the dragon and said, "That was a little arrow and it only hurt you a little bit. But if you annoy my friends again, I shall come back with a really big bow and arrow."

The dragon ran away and was never seen again.
And all the people in the village shouted
together, "Hurrah for the little princess! Hurrah!
The dragon has run away. Hurrah! Hurrah!"

The little princess was glad that she had been able to help the villagers. She said good-bye to everyone and set off on her journey once more. She walked on and on, through three more forests, over two more mountains, and across another lonely desert, until she came to another village. Since she was hungry, she decided to buy some bread with her gold coin. But there was nothing to eat in the village. Even the baker had no flour for making bread.

"If only I could get at that flour," said the baker sadly, pointing to a heap of bulging sacks tied firmly with silk ribbon.

"Nobody can open them," said the baker, "because a magician cast a spell on the sacks that made the knots too tight to undo."

"The knots may be too tight for your great big hands to undo, but perhaps not for mine," said the little princess.

She went over to the sacks and with her little fingers undid the ribbons until all the sacks were open.

Then the baker was able to bake bread for the whole village, and some for Little Princess Leonora, too, who paid him with her gold coin.

The villagers were hungry no longer, and shouted all together, "Hurrah! Long live the little princess! Now we have enough to eat. Hurrah! Hurrah!"

The little princess was glad that she had been able to help the villagers. She walked on and on, through three more forests, over two more mountains, and across yet another lonely desert until she came to a village where the people were terrorized by a flock of vultures.

"Every day at three o'clock the vultures descend on our village," they told her. "And no one dares to chase them away."

"I will go," said Little Princess Leonora.

"But you are so little!" exclaimed everyone.

Little Princess Leonora did not stop to listen to their protests, but as she scrambled up the rocky mountainside she wondered how she would manage this time.

When she reached the top of the mountain, and could see the vultures clearly for the first time, she realized how incredibly ugly they were. In fact, they were so ugly that there and then she had an idea for frightening them away. She took her mirror and went right up to the king vulture, which was the ugliest of them all.

He stretched out his long neck to see what the little princess was holding.

When he saw his reflection in the mirror, and realized how ugly he was, he flapped his wings and flew away in fright as fast as he could. And all the other vultures followed him.

"So you were afraid of yourself, were you?" murmured the little princess.

Down on the plain below, the people saw the vultures flying
off and shouted all together, "Hurrah! Long live the little princess!
The vultures have gone. Hurrah! Hurrah!"

Now Little Princess Leonora felt a little lost and afraid as she sat all alone on the mountain peak. She was very small and the whole wide world seemed to be spread out below her. Then she remembered the candy that the Queen Mother had given her. She untied her bundle, felt around inside it, found a candy and ate it.

It was good, but it was not enough.

So she fished out another candy.

It was very good, but it was not enough.

So she fished out the final candy.

And even though she was so small and had the whole wide world spread out below her, as she sucked that last candy, she began to feel better.

So she set her crown firmly on her head and set off once more, but this time she made for home.

Again she crossed deserts, mountains, and forests, and yet more deserts, mountains, and forests. Altogether she crossed three deserts, climbed over six mountains, and made her way through nine forests. And as she passed through the villages that she had rescued, everywhere she heard people shouting, "Hurrah for the little princess! Hurrah! Hurrah!"

They shouted so loudly that the sound of their voices reached as far as the court of the Queen Mother.

When Little Princess Leonora arrived home, she was met by the joyful cries of the children, "Hurrah! Long live the little princess! Welcome home!"

And they all shouted loudly so that she could hear, "She is braver than a hundred knights on horseback!"

The Queen Mother leaned out of a castle window and waved to the little princess.

"She is even more courageous than her grandfather," she thought, "because anyone can go off to war. But to be such a brave little princess you need a special kind of courage..."

"Welcome home!"

For Tomaso, who gave me the idea for the vultures and the mirror
— B.M.

For Leonardo and his grandmother Luz
— O.M.

Barefoot Books
37 West 17th Street
4th Floor East
New York, New York 10011

© 1999 Edizioni Arka – Milano/Italy

First published in Italy by Edizioni Arka in 1999.
This edition published in the United States of America in 2000 by Barefoot Books Ltd.

This book was typeset in Leawood Book 12.5pt on 20pt leading

Translated by Diana Handley
Typesetting of the US edition by Design/Section, Frome, England
Color separation by Fotoriproduzioni Grafiche E. Beverari, Verona, Italy
Printed in Hong Kong/China by South China Printing Co. (1988) Ltd.

This book has been printed on 100% acid-free paper

ISBN 1 84148 267 6

U.S. Cataloging-in-Publication Data (Library of Congress Standards)

Masini, Beatrice.
    A brave little princess / written by Beatrice Masini ; illustrated by Octavia Monaco.
[32]p. : col. ill. ;   cm.
Originally published: Italy: Edizioni Arka, 1999.
Summary: Little Princess Leonora is laughed at because she is so small,
but with great courage and special gifts from her grandmother, she sets
out to face a dragon, a sorcerer's spell, and a flock of hungry vultures.
ISBN 1-84148-267-6
1. Courage -- Fiction. 2. Size -- Fiction. I. Monaco, Octavia, ill. II. Title.
[E] 21   1999   AC   CIP

1 3 5 7 9 8 6 4 2

walk
the way of  wonder...
# Barefoot Books

The barefoot child symbolizes the human being who is in harmony
with the natural world and moves freely across boundaries of many kinds.
Barefoot Books explores this image with a range of high-quality picture books
for children of all ages. We work with artists, writers and storytellers from
many cultures, focusing on themes that encourage independence of spirit,
promote understanding and acceptance of different traditions,
and foster a life-long love of learning.
www.barefoot-books.com